NORTHANGER ABBEY

NORTHANGER ABBEY

Jane Austen

WORDSWORTH CLASSICS

This edition published 1993 by
Wordsworth Editions Limited
Cumberland House, Crib Street
Ware, Hertfordshire SG12 9ET

ISBN 1 85326 043 6

Typeset by Antony Gray
Printed and bound in Great Britain by
Mackays of Chatham plc, Chatham, Kent